Waltham Forest Public Libraries

PS168

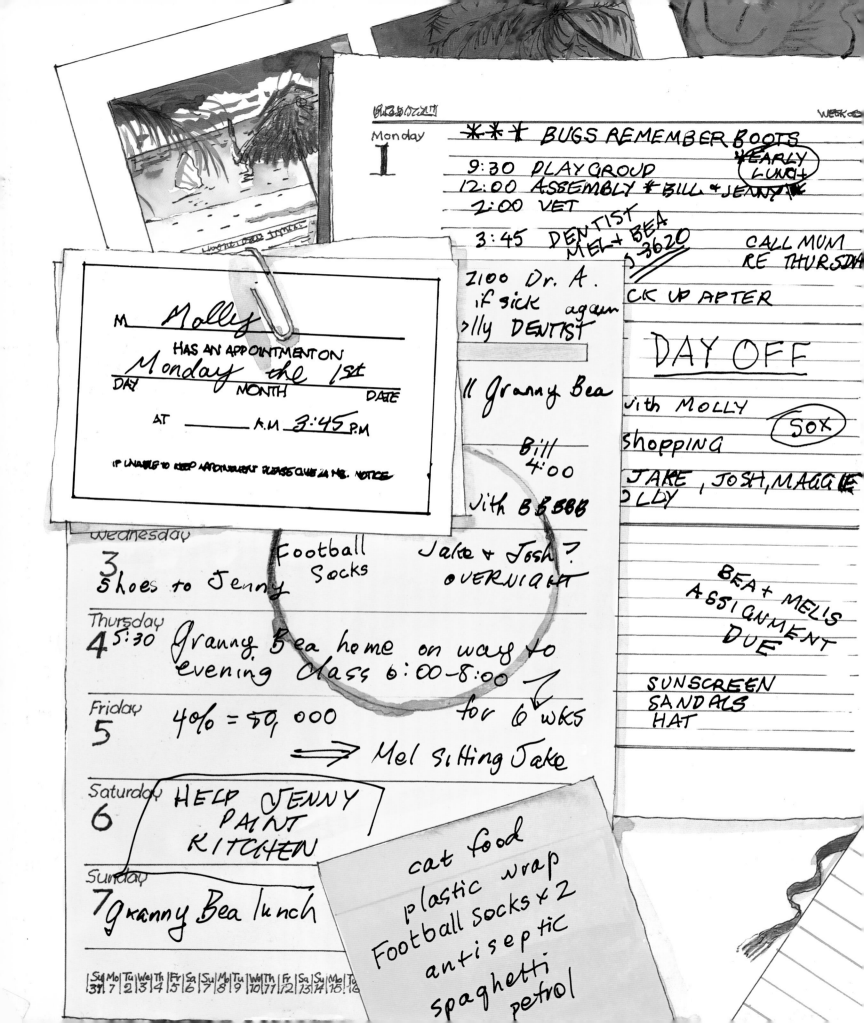

1998
Thursday 4 — PLUMBER

B. BACK LATE

1:00 CLINIC

MUM!

MAGGIE WILL

JENNY PICKUP 9:00

Friday 5 — PICK UP

CANCEL MAIL

ASK MICKY & JAKE TO FEED AN

6:00 BE

BILL 12:

Saturday 6 — (FILM)

Sunday 7

REPORT DUE 31/6

BLUE MIST VINYL
MOONSHADOW EGG SHELL
DROP CLOTHS

MONDAY 1
PICK UP DRY CLEANING

DAY OFF   ASSEMBLY 12:00
JAKE CIRCUS 3:45-4:15
BUGS FOOTBALL 4:30
BEGIN WORK AT 6:30 ——— 8:30

JAKE & JOSH TO BIDDIE 5:00 SUPPER

DRY CLEANING !!!

ER WITH H. ♡

TO MAGGIE TO SLEEP

PICK UP J. FROM MUSIC LESSON
6:30
8:30   4:00 TEA AT BIDDIE'S

WERS FOR B & B

BIKE SERVICE
W 5:30-11:30   MELE BEA TO IT

WITH BILL
PAINT KITCHEN

JOSH PICK UP BIKE 11:15

GET KEY FROM
BIDDIE ⊕ AL-LEAVING 10:30 ISH

E. MIND J TO FEED RABBIT & G. P.S

BLUE MIST
ROLLER REPLACEMENT
SMALL BRUSH

DOG FOOD
CAT FOOD
PLANT FOOD
FURNITURE POLISH
MUSIC WORKBOOK

JAM
BIKE BELL
COCOA
CHIPS
COKE

HOW TO RESTORE WOOD
PUBLISHED BY DORSEY HEAD

JUGGLING BALLS

CLEANIN

Bill
Biddie
Bea
Bugs
Boo Boo + Bear
Granny Bea

For Frances
J.O.

A Red Fox Book

Published by Random House Children's Books
20 Vauxhall Bridge Road, London SW1V 2SA

A division of The Random House Group Ltd
London Melbourne Sydney Auckland Johannesburg and agencies throughout the world

Copyright © Jan Ormerod 1998

1 3 5 7 9 10 8 6 4 2

First published in Great Britain by The Bodley Head Children's Books 1998
Red Fox edition 2000

Printed in Singapore by Tien Wah Press (PTE) Ltd

THE RANDOM HOUSE GROUP Limited Reg. No. 954009
www.randomhouse.co.uk

ISBN 0-09-926289-4

Jan Ormerod

Who's Who In Our Street?

JENNY
JOSH
JAKE
JOCK

Maggie
Me
Micky + Molly

RED FOX

Breakfast here,

lunch there,

and over here for tea.

Jump down, Cat!
You belong to us all in our street.

It's Monday morning. Schooltime.

Josh is a racer.

Moll and Bugs are lazy bones.

Mel and Bea chatter and natter, but they do keep an
eye on Micky and Jake.
There's always someone to walk with in our street.

Micky's sick and Maggie is at work,
so Biddie and Boo Boo take him home.

At school, Mel, Bea and Josh sing,
and at work, Maggie gives Granny Bea a ring.

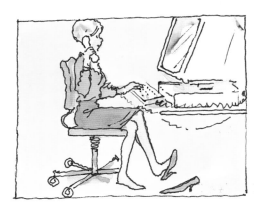

'Come to lunch
on Sunday?'

After school, Jenny takes Jake to circus class.

Then she posts the letters, pays the bills,
collects the cleaning
and buys a book for Micky.
Don't forget the apples for Biddie.
Don't forget Bugs.

Football is finished!
Someone is always lending a hand on our street.

Mel and Bea take Molly to the dentist,
then do homework.

Josh is watching the telly.
Someone is being lazy on our street - and we all know who that is!

It's Tuesday, after school. Bugs plays with Molly.
Maggie kisses her better when she
scrapes her knee.

Micky plays with Jock while
Jake practises the piano.
Josh is trying to watch the telly.

Bugs, Molly and Boo Boo look after the pets
while Maggie and Bill go shopping.

The big girls are doing homework (and this time it's true).
Biddie will help them if they need her.

Nearly time to eat.
The cheese needs grating.
The table needs laying.
The shopping needs unpacking.
Who's being helpful on our street?

And whose turn is it to wash up?

On Wednesday night, when Jenny goes out
she wears Biddie's skirt and Maggie's shoes.
Who paints her nails?
Who puts on her make up?

And who gets the most excited?

On Thursday Granny Bea visits with a hat for Boo Boo.
Molly sits on her lap. Jake shows her his juggling.
Bugs has painted a picture, and Mel and Bea have made a cake.

Who do we love to see in our street?

On Fridays, when Jenny works late,

Jake sometimes sleeps here,
or sometimes sleeps here.

Tonight, Josh is in charge,
and Mel and Bea are helping out.

Who is looking after whom?
And who ate Jock's supper?

When Mel, Micky and Molly go to their dad's for the weekend,
Maggie may go for a walk in the sun

'Hi Mel, it's me!'

or the rain.

Who gets the muddiest?

Some weekends Bill keeps an eye on everyone
while the mums do the garden.
(They like doing that in our street.)

This Saturday, Bill takes Bugs, Boo Boo, Molly, Micky,
Jake and Jock to the park to play while Biddie has a rest.
Mel and Bea do homework, and Josh watches the telly.

Maggie helps Jenny. 'That looks better.'
Who is most tired at the end of the day?

Bad dog, Jock! That naughty cat!
Maggie shouts and Jenny cries.
Bugs and Molly get the giggles.
Jake and Micky get cross.
Boo Boo screams.
And Mel and Bea come running.

Josh makes everyone a mug of tea and cleans up.

Who's a good boy, then?

It's Sunday. Bill, Biddie, Bea, Bugs and Boo Boo are off on holiday.

Who has lunch with Granny Bea?
Who waters the plants?

Who cuddles the rabbit? Who cleans out the guinea pigs?

Who misses their friends?

DEAR ALL —
WE MISS YOU I
WISH YOU WERE
HERE. THE BEACH
IS GREAT!
LOTS OF LOVE —
BIDDIE   X
BILL   X
BEA   X
BUGS   X X
BOO BOO   X
(and BEAR) X

MAGGIE, MEL, MICKY,
MOLLY, JENNY, JOSH,
JAKE, JOCK + CAT
c/o MRS. BLUE
19 THE AVENUE
BROOKLANDS

And who is pleased to be back together at the end of the week?

All of us
in our street!

Monday
15

9:30 PLAYGROUP *BOOTS! BUGS

MUM TO SIT STAY OVER
DINNER JENNY + 1+ — 7:0

Monday
15

dinner Jenny's 7:30 —
meet H/
Mel + Bea baby sitting   # chocs
10:30 Coffee Jenny
2:00 bank Manager
3:45 Melly + Bugs to part

6:00-8:00 computer class

to father's 6:30
Biddie + Bill to

mum—
I'm sorry I
was grumpy!
love,
Mel

Lae
Thursday
18

3 YDS. LINING FABRIC

MONDAY
15 DAY OFF   8:45 CIRCUS   DRY
           PICK UP BUGS 4:30 CLEANING
BIDDIE, BILL, MAGGIE, H TO DINNER 7:30ish

ESDAY   WORK 5:30-8:30
         OFFEE WITH MAGGIE
           J & W TO BIDDIE 5:00

         BORROW BIDDIE'S
           SEWING MACHINE

Sunday

chips
BLUE THREAD
COKE
AVOCADOS
MUSTARD
PARSLEY

HOW TO LINE CURTAINS?
BIDDIE'S MUM

Some bestselling Red Fox picture books

THE BIG ALFIE AND ANNIE ROSE STORYBOOK
by Shirley Hughes
OLD BEAR
by Jane Hissey
OI! GET OFF OUR TRAIN
by John Burningham
DON'T DO THAT!
by Tony Ross
NOT NOW, BERNARD
by David McKee
ALL JOIN IN
by Quentin Blake
THE WHALES' SONG
by Gary Blythe and Dyan Sheldon
JESUS' CHRISTMAS PARTY
by Nicholas Allan
THE PATCHWORK CAT
by Nicola Bayley and William Mayne
WILLY AND HUGH
by Anthony Browne
THE WINTER HEDGEHOG
by Ann and Reg Cartwright
A DARK, DARK TALE
by Ruth Brown
HARRY, THE DIRTY DOG
by Gene Zion and Margaret Bloy Graham
DR XARGLE'S BOOK OF EARTHLETS
by Jeanne Willis and Tony Ross
WHERE'S THE BABY?
by Pat Hutchins